David Melling was born in Oxford.
His first book was shortlisted for the Smarties
Book Award and The Kiss that Missed was
shortlisted for the Kate Greenaway Award.
He is married and lives with his wife
and children in Oxfordshire.

www.davidmelling.co.uk

Look
out for
all the
GOBLINS
books:

Stone Goblins
Tree Goblins
Puddle Goblins
Shadow Goblins

shadow GOBLINS

David Melling

Hodder
Children's
Books

A division of Hachette Children's Books

The ᴉstrator
e

A Catalogue record for this book is available from the British Library

ISBN-13: 978 0 340 93051 9

Printed and bound in Germany by GGP Media GmbH, Pößneck

The paper and board used in this paperback by Hodder Children's Books are
natural recyclable products made from wood grown in sustainable forests.
The manufacturing processes conform to the environmental
regulations of the country of origin.

Hodder Children's Books
A division of Hachette Children's Books
338 Euston Road, London NW1 3BH
An Hachette Livre UK Company

Fingerprints by Monika and Luka Melling

For Luka

THE
TREE OF SHADOWS

Path from "Who knows Where"

Black

Shadow Goblins are shape changers. Yep, you guessed it, they change shape and cause all sorts of "nasties" in Black Wood.

Black Wood? Well, that's where they live. A dark and terrible wood with the type of creatures that make you want to say, "please don't eat me."

And if that lot isn't bad enough, you're more than likely to be chased by a shadow with no body. Everyone's worst nightmare.

Enjoy!

Introducing the
Shadow Goblins

Murkbag

A Night Teacher, or *Shade*, as he likes to be
called. Doesn't like the kind of spooky shapes
knocking about in Black Wood. Gets flappy
when scared!

Pungent

Brave when he has to be, but he is hopeless at animal hand shadows, and so must suffer the humiliation of wearing a rabbit costume.

Stinglip

Pungent's best friend and only classmate. He can be a little nervous of things that go bump in the night. Not so good if you're a Shadow Goblin.

Bone-zzz

A Shadow Goblin who had an accident. Now
he is a talking skeleton … with *no* shadow,
just a fly for company, buzzing around inside
his bones. A little sad, he spends his nights
searching for his lost shadow.

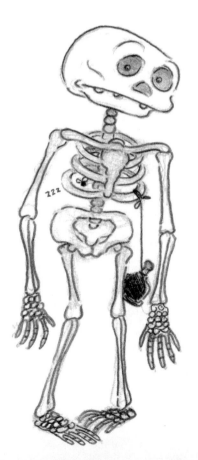

Monkey Goblin

The Monkey Goblin is a rare kind of goblin and a
bit of a loner. She is fussily tidy and loves to work.
Present employment: Arranger of Inkpots in
The Tree of Shadows.

A FEW FACTS ABOUT SHADOW GOBLINS

HABITS AND HABITAT

Black Wood

A dark moody kind of place, with trees that pinch and creatures that make you want to say, "Please don't eat me." There is almost no light of any kind, but you can always find shadows in Black Wood. And if you're not looking at them, they'll be looking at you!

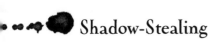 Shadow-Stealing

Shadow Goblins have the ability to steal other creatures' shadows. Goblin magic! They do this by turning the shadow into ink and drinking it! They love to play dark, naughty tricks on the other creatures of the woods. And sometimes, if they are cross enough, on each other!

Shape-shifting

Shadow Goblins can change shape, into the creature whose shadow they have been drinking. This is called *shape-shifting*. The effect *usually* wears off by the end of the night …

THE ART OF LIFTING SHADOWS

Please note: Shadow Goblins love picking on sheep, and so for the purpose of the following explanation the "victim" will be a sheep.

Black Shadow Gloves

These are used to
hypnotise the sheep by

clever use of hand shadows. Rabbit shapes work best.

The Ibble Obble Song and the Rabbit Hop
Very silly song and dance that must be done together. For beginners who are rubbish at hand shadows.

♩ Ibble

obble

Black,

Bobble

Ibble

obble

OUT!

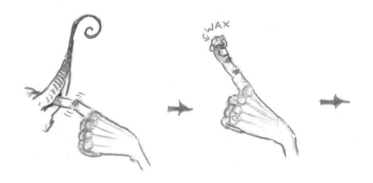

Silver Trail

Once the sheep is hypnotised, a Shadow Goblin
will scoop out its own earwax with a finger and
trace around the outline of the shadow. This will
form a silver-trailed crust.

Inking

Pour ink into the shadow, right up to the silver-trailed outline. The ink will not go over this line.

Inkpotting

Within minutes, the ink will evaporate, rising upward into a plume of smoke which is then drawn into the inkpot, like a genie into a lamp.

Once "corked" inside the inkpot, the shadow will slowly turn back into a thick, sticky black ink called gloop. It is now ready to drink.

THE ART OF SHAPE-SHIFTING

Drinking Shadows

The Shadow Goblin who drinks the gloop
will turn into the shape of the sheep. This is
usually a gradual process. Before the change
is complete the goblin may take on some of
the sheep's characteristics – nibbling grass,
bleating, etc.

Shape-shifting is a peculiar process best
described here with pictures …

THREE FAVOURITE SHADOW GOBLIN TRICKS

1. Knotted sheep tails – Why Shadow Goblins like to pick on sheep so much is unclear – maybe because they're probably the easiest creature to trick. Although it has been known for Shadow Goblins to tie knots in the hair of sleeping children.

2. Shadow Swapping – A sheep could wake up with a rabbit shadow, or a rabbit could wake up with a sheep shadow.

3. Double Shadows – An argument between two shadow goblins can result in one of them ending up with two shadows. It may not sound *so* bad, but it would be like you waking up one morning with two noses.

HOW TO SPOT A SHAPE-SHIFTER

You may come across a sheep, for example, and think nothing of it. But how do you know – I mean, *really* know – that the sheep you're looking at is not a goblin in disguise? Answer: step on their shadow!

Sticky Shadows

If any object is placed on a sheep's shadow, one of two things will happen. Either the sheep will try to nibble it and eventually wander off. Or the shadow will become stuck under the weight of the object – and if this happens, it means it is a Shadow Goblin, who will be unable to move away until the night is over, leaving plenty of time for you to run away.

MURKBAG'S SHADOW-SPOTTING GUIDE TO BLACK WOOD

Run away

Run away

Run away

Food

Kick

Run away

OTHER BITS AND BOBS

Shadow Goblin Ink

A stolen shadow, once bottled, turns into a thick, sticky black gloop. It takes around ten minutes and smells like warmed-up earwax.

Ink-spots

The sight of ink-spots on the forest floor is a sure sign of Shadow Goblin activity!

Inkpots

Inkpots come in different shapes and sizes. When a shadow has been *potted* it is corked and labelled, ready for *The Tree of Shadows*.

The Tree of Shadows

An old wreck of a tree, hollow and riddled with holes, it is used as a sort of *library* of shadows. Shadow Goblins can come here if they feel like a change of shape! The Monkey Goblin, Arranger of Inkpots, is in charge of lending out the inkpots.

A Closer look inside (and around) the Robe of Darkness

Eyes – Excellent eyesight in both day and night.

Badges of Horror – Like cub-scout badges, they have to earn them.

Torch – Part of the hypnotising kit.

Curly-Wurly Shoes – Fashionable, they match the curly ears and robe.

Black Gloves – Used to aid
Hand Shadows.

Inkpots and Secret Pockets – A robe has many
hidden pockets, some so large it would seem
impossible. But the robe is a mysterious and
magical thing, capable of all manner of curiosities!

Contents

The Story Begins ...

The sheep couldn't sleep. They weren't sure why, only that it didn't feel like a good time to have their eyes closed. They huddled together, but not for warmth – being a sheep was toasty warm because they had their own woolly jumper. No, there was something about the night.

Some*thing*, somewhere, was giving them all the heebie-jeebies!

A shadow suddenly broke cover on the far side of the field and flickered towards them across the grass like a black ghost. The sheep were terrified, unable to move.

Their wild eyes watched in horror.

Sheep are often slow to reach a decision, but on this night they all agreed to be somewhere else as quickly as possible. They fled, clumsily and bumpily but still huddled together, like a cloud on legs.

All except one, a small ewe. She stood rooted to the spot.

The shadow stopped right in front of her, hovering. It was a strange, shapeless shadow, a patch of darkness curling like black smoke. It looked down at the ewe and the ewe looked up at the shadow.

The rest of the flock had reached the far end of the field. They could just make out the ewe, briefly, before the shadow covered her, a blanket of bad dreams.

There was no sound, no sound at all. And after a moment there was no ewe, no shadow … nothing.

It wasn't until the sun was high in the sky the following morning that the other sheep had the courage to shuffle over and have a look.

There, perched on the grass, was a small black inkpot.

Chapter One

Murkbag's First Day

"My name is Murkbag, and I'll be your Shade for this evening."

Two little Shadow Goblins got to their feet and chorused, "Good evening, Mr Murkbag," and then sat down.

Murkbag smiled down at his class of two goblins. It was his first time as Night Teacher and he wanted to make a good impression, so he was wearing his longest, blackest cloak. Lots of swishing, that's the ticket, he thought.

He paced in front of them, changing direction suddenly and with purpose, his cloak billowing out behind him like a large shadow.

"Now, we have three nights! In that time you will learn how to hand-shadow, shadow-steal and shape-shift."

Murkbag paused and shot his pupils a sly look. One was yawning, and the other was picking at something he'd rather not think about. Murkbag frowned, cleared his throat and decided to turn up the volume.

"Tonight is the night!" he said dramatically,

raising his hands. Both goblins jumped to attention. "And these here fingers," he gave them a wiggle, "are going to help make you Shadow Goblins to remember!"

He looked down at their blank faces. Turning quickly, he swept up his cloak and swirled it in a way that suggested magic, mischief and mayhem.

"Why do you keep flapping your dress around?" asked the taller goblin, Pungent.

Murkbag stopped suddenly. "I'm *not* flapping, and it *isn't* a dress!" he said stiffly.

"My mum's got one just like that and *she* calls it a dress," said Pungent defiantly.

"Mine too," said the other goblin.

The two goblins agreed, nodding to each other, before turning back to Murkbag.

Murkbag leaned forward and tried to smile.

"Your name," he said to Pungent, "I know. But this fellow here has yet to introduce himself."

"Stinglip, sir."

"Really," said Murkbag. "An unusual name. Well, *Mister* Stinglip, perhaps a little less talking and a little more listening ... hmm?"

"Y'sir."

Murkbag smiled again and stepped back. He felt the first few minutes – so important when starting a new class – were not going particularly well. He coughed and tried again.

"In a moment, I will be giving you your shape-shifting starter packs." The goblins cooed. That's better, Murkbag thought. "Then we will go a little deeper into Black Wood and find a place called Goat's Log. Here, we will—"

Stinglip's hand shot up in to the air. "Why's it called Goat's Log?"

"Because it's a funny-looking log that looks like a goat?" suggested Pungent.

"Exactly," said Murkbag. "Thank you, Pungent! Now, where was I? Ah yes, we will be—"

"Does that mean if there's a log that looks like a dress it would be called Dress's Log?" said Stinglip, looking at Murkbag's cloak. Pungent giggled.

Murkbag wrestled with his temper. What I need to do, he thought, is show them who's boss.

He took a deep breath, opened both arms out and began waving them like a giant bat.

"**Your cloak will become part of you, part of your shadow,**" he boomed. "And when you learn to use them properly, the shapes you take on will baffle your enemy, confuse your friends and maybe, one day, save your life!" With a hiss and a twirl, he hopped on one leg and turned around three times.

In truth, the swishy black cloak had little to do with anything, but he felt it set the right tone and, usually, grabbed their attention. Murkbag paused, his eyes closed. An impressive silence. An impressive display! Yes, he thought, they were listening now! He smiled again. Then, he heard whispering.

"My mum's got the same frilly pockets, can you see?"

"Yeah, my dad says you only get pockets with girl cloaks."

"This is *not* a dress," Murkbag gargled. "It's a *Robe of Darkness*, and these are *not* pockets, they're *Badges of Horror*! Any pockets you may see – though I'll thank you *not* to look inside my robe – are very useful pockets for things like, um, my sandwiches. And there are *no* frilly bits *at all*!"

He glared down at them and was pleased to see they were suitably shocked, although the bit about sandwiches had spoilt it a little.

"At *last!*" snarled Murkbag pacing around, "a sense of respect for your teacher, and—"

A dress-shaped paper dart sailed past his head.

"*Right*, who threw that?" snapped Murkbag. He swung round just a little too quickly, caught his foot in the folds of his cloak, and pitched forward. He landed on his nose, the cloak gently draping over him like a collapsed tent.

For a second there was complete silence.

But Murkbag knew they would laugh … and they did, long and loud.

He sighed. In a weak voice, muffled by the cloak, he said, "OK, let's take a five-minute break – class dismissed."

Goat's Log

Untangled, but still a little flustered, Murkbag
led his pupils moodily into Black Wood,
along a dry, cracked path.

All three were soon gathered around Goat's
Log which, Pungent and Stinglip had to agree,
did look remarkably like a goat.

"Now then, um … are we all ready for, er …"
Murkbag began. His confidence had been
bruised a little, but he was determined to

press on.

"It is no coincidence that we are here tonight under the guiding light of a full moon, so we won't be, er … needing a torch. You will note this log's shadow, and pay particular attention to its shape."

He winced, hoping neither one of them would mention anything about dresses, and was pleased to see that the atmosphere of Black Wood appeared to have made them forget all about it. Indeed, Pungent and Stinglip were listening very closely.

"In a moment I will be giving you your shadow-stealing kits," said Murkbag, "but first I will show you how to separate this log from its shadow. Now stand well back," he declared. "Watch and learn!"

Lesson 1: The Cunning Art
of Shadow-Stealing

Murkbag walked a short distance away, all
the time fumbling around with the inside
of his cloak. Pungent and Stinglip looked at each
other and shrugged. They couldn't see what he
was doing.

When Murkbag turned to face them, he held
up his hands with a hopeful grin. He was wearing
a pair of fluffy black gloves about three sizes too
big. After waving them round for a moment, he
strolled casually towards the log. He stopped a
little way away and checked the moon's position,
making sure his shadow stretched out before him.

Suddenly he let out a hiss and waggled his hands furiously, and the shadow of a rabbit appeared, dancing on the goat's wooden face.

Then he dashed around to the shadow side of the log and, taking one glove off, he stuck a finger in his right ear and had a good root around. Using the same finger, he traced around the outline of the shadow, which the goblins noticed left a silver trail like that of a snail.

Still working quickly, Murkbag rummaged around inside his cloak again and produced a small glass inkpot. He uncorked it and emptied the contents, a thick black ink, over the shadow. There seemed to be more ink inside than the inkpot could possibly hold, but still it came pouring out, staying within the silver-trailed outline until, at last, the entire shadow was a glistening puddle.

Suddenly, and much to the surprise of Pungent and Stinglip, Murkbag gathered his robes up around his waist, revealing long thin legs, and began to sing the Ibble Obble song and dance to the Rabbit Hop!

"Ibble, Obble,
Black Bobble,
Ibble, Obble, *OUT!*"

Almost immediately the ink began drying. A thin line of black smoke curled upwards, gathering into a cloud just above the ground. As it grew in size, it took on the shape of Goat's Log. When the shadow was complete, it swirled around quickly, getting smaller and smaller before disappearing into Murkbag's inkpot like a genie into its lamp.

Pungent and Stinglip looked down at the ground, where the shadow had been. There was nothing except the silver-trailed outline, which was already fading.

The whole thing had taken no more than three minutes.

Murkbag corked the inkpot, smiled, took a low bow and said, "Any questions?"

Pungent had a question.

Murkbag's smile stiffened and he frowned slightly.

"Well, *yes,* if you must. Behind that tree over there, but don't be long."

Lesson 2: Hand Shadows or Rabbit Costumes?

After Murkbag's demonstration, the three Shadow Goblins ate some beetle-wing crackers. Then Murkbag handed out the shadow-stealing kits, each bound in deep purple velvet sacks. Inside they found:

– a pair of fluffy black gloves

– a torch-hat (with head strap)

– an inkpot

– the Rabbit's Hop songsheet and stepping guide

– a dark leather-bound book titled:

Hand-Shadow with Confidence

(All the shapes with none of the worry)

"Hand shadows," continued Murkbag, "are a clever way of hypnotising your victim – and for some reason, rabbit hand shadows work best. Once you have hypnotised the victim, you have only a few minutes to separate the shadow from the animal before they wake. And if they wake up it's all over, because the same animal can't be hypnotised more than once a night."

"And why are we stealing shadows, again?" asked Pungent, who was trying to put his gloves on backwards.

Murkbag blinked. "I would have thought," he said, "you would know that answer yourself, no?" One look at their faces told him otherwise. "We Shadow Goblins like to steal other creatures' shadows, so we can drink the ink and change into the shape of that creature. And once we've changed shape … we do what we do best."

He bounced his eyebrows, but still their faces looked empty.

"Tricks!" said Murkbag. "We like to play tricks!"

Stinglip could do a rabbit hand shadow almost at once, with two floppy ears and everything. So he went straight on to dance the Rabbit's Hop, which meant: lots of dancing, hopping, trying not to get too dizzy and fall over, while singing a silly song.

Pungent, on the other hand, could only manage a shape they all agreed looked like a stick-swallowing slug.

He tried and tried, his arms ached and his fingers ached, but still he couldn't do it.

Eventually, Murkbag raised his hands and said, "Stop! I'm, er … sorry, Pungent, but for now you'll have to wear a costume."

"A costume?"

"Yes, a rabbit costume. A bit plonky, I'll admit, but until you can get the hang of the hand shadow it's the only way we can continue the lesson. The night's half gone already and we have to steal a shadow before dawn. Most goblins, I may add, can do the hand shadow bit in five minutes!"

He turned his back on them and started fussing around inside his robe again.

"Aha!" he said. Twirling around, he pulled out the rabbit costume, the way a magician would

do from his top hat. "Here we are! There's only one size – but it should fit. You'll be fine!"

Pungent groaned.

Inside Black Wood

The rabbit costume was a little pinchy around the edges, and they had trouble with the zips, but eventually Pungent stood miserably in front of a long fold-out mirror Murkbag had also produced from his robe.

"Perfect!" said Murkbag brightly. "Now then, we need to move on to shadow-stealing. Which means a short walk, um …" he scratched his head, "this way, I think."

Pungent looked gloomily at the trees ahead. He didn't like them. They were thicker here and more tightly packed. They were the type of trees, thought Pungent, that wouldn't move out the way,

27

no matter how nicely you asked.

Stinglip, on the other hand, was looking forward to the adventure.

"Cheer up!" he said, looking over at Pungent. "It could be worse."

"Worse? *How?*" The rabbit costume was so tight Pungent found the easiest way to move was by hopping.

Stinglip watched him quietly and then pulled a face. "Yeah well, fair enough!"

Murkbag led the way until eventually they came to a small scratchy field.

A wooden fence was relaxing its borders in the tall grass. A rambling mess of broken planks and gaps, it saw no reason to smarten itself up at the sudden appearance of three Shadow Goblins.

Murkbag stopped and brought a finger to his lips. "Sssh! Now, I want you to be very quiet."

He crouched down to their level. "In this field you'll find a flock of sheep. Now sheep are, without doubt, the dippiest animal you'll meet, and therefore the easiest to hypnotise.

One look at that rabbit hand shadow of yours, Stinglip, or, um … your costume, Pungent, and … er … they'll be *all* yours!

"I want you to go in there and bring me back a sheep shadow … in *this*!" He held up a small inkpot and gave it a wiggle. Pungent and Stinglip took it in turns to speak:

"Who …?"

"What …?"

"How …?"

"When …?

"Now, now, don't be like that!" said Murkbag. "You have everything you need in your kits. If you work as a team you should be in and out of there in no more than ten minutes!"

"Who …?"

"What …?"

"How …?"

"When …?"

Murkbag ignored their protests. "Pungent,
you wear the torch and stand behind Stinglip.
And, um … Stinglip, you do the hand shadows
and then together, well … let's just see how you
get on. Oh, and Pungent – don't forget these."

"Carrots?" blinked Pungent.

31

"Yes, they're part of the costume. You have to put two of them in your mouth. Like fangs, see?"

Pungent groaned again.

"Don't worry, it's only during the hand shadow bit, then you can take them out!"

"Where are *you* going?" Stinglip managed to ask.

"I'll be right here, watching! I'm not allowed to come in the field with you or it won't be a proper test."

"Test?" they squeaked.

"Ssssh! *Please!* Now go, before you wake up all the sheep. And believe me, you don't want to do that!"

He gave them an encouraging shove and watched them shuffle forward into the dark, dark night.

Sheep-Shadow-Stealing!

Pungent and Stinglip squinted around the field for any sign of life. At last, Stinglip pointed to what looked like some sort of giant sponge, packed tightly in the far corner, which they guessed correctly were the sheep.

Pungent was fumbling with the torch. He couldn't tell if the moon was out or not, but this far inside Black Wood it made little difference. Stinglip was close behind, quietly practising his rabbit shapes.

As they drew nearer they slowed up and tried to pick out a single sheep. But in this darkness it was hopeless and they were forced to move closer and closer. At any moment they expected the flock to panic and scatter.

It was only when they were so close they could reach out and touch the sheep that Pungent and Stinglip knew there was something wrong. The sheep were *not* asleep. They were trembling uncontrollably, their eyes open, wild and terrified.

Pungent and Stinglip turned around nervously, hoping to see that Murkbag had followed them and was standing

close by, ready to help.

But he wasn't.

"W-what shall we do?" asked Stinglip,

trying to
stop his teeth
chattering.

"Beats m-me,"
said Pungent. "But we've
come this far. L-let's just do it
and get out of here."

He held up the torch.

"Hang on, Stinglip!" he said suddenly. "What
are we doing? I don't think the sheep need
hypnotising. They're not moving at all – not even
blinking. They're scared stiff!" He waved a
gloved hand in front of their faces.

"This is w-weird!" mumbled Stinglip.

They walked carefully around the flock. The sheep were clearly in some kind of trance – a clump of sheep with nowhere to go!

Then Pungent spotted a single sheep a little away from the others.

"T-this one'll do," he said.

"Do you think we *should*?" said Stinglip. "I mean, you know … with them being the way they are?"

"Why not? If we – hey, wait a minute – where's the sheep's shadow gone?"

"W-w-what do you mean, w-w-where's the …?"

They looked at each other.

"Shine the torch properly," said Stinglip. "You know, the way Murkbag showed us."

"I *am*!" said Pungent.

"Well then, where's the shadow?"

"This is *really* weird. Wait a minute – what's *that*?"

There, sitting quietly, was a small inkpot. The grass around it was speckled with black spots.

Both goblins noticed that the inkpot was similar in shape and size to the one Murkbag had given them.

Stinglip picked it up carefully and gave it a shake.

"It's full!" He thought for a minute. "You don't think the sheep's shadow is in *here*, do you?"

"It must be!" said Pungent.

They looked for the silver trail but there was nothing, so they turned back to look at the sheep's face again. Pungent shone the torch into one eye and then the other. It blinked once but made no other sign of any kind. It just stood there, staring out into the darkness.

"Maybe this is what they look like when they've lost their shadow," said Pungent. "You reckon?"

"I dunno," frowned Stinglip. "Something just isn't right about this whole thing." He looked across at the other sheep. "Is it me, or has it just got a lot colder?"

Pungent was about to agree when a movement caught his eye. Something came floating out of the trees and skittled past them.

"W-w-what was *that*?" they said together.

"I vote we take this inkpot," said Stinglip quickly. "Old Murkbag won't notice the difference. We tell him we've done it, and get out of here – what d'you think?"

Pungent didn't need asking twice. He threw the torch over his shoulder and together they ran back through the darkness to where they had left Murkbag.

"Where have you *been*?" asked Murkbag, a

little too quickly.
"I mean, h-how
did you get on, all
right?"

Stinglip guiltily
showed him the
inkpot.

"Excellent!"
sighed Murkbag.
"Now, let's get out
of here quic—!"
He coughed and said, "I mean, um … when
you're ready, er, shall we go?"

It was an Accident!

Murkbag bustled his pupils away from the
field, back through the wooden
darkness. It wasn't long before the trees thinned
a little, the blackness turned a smudgy grey and
once again they could see each other properly
without pulling funny faces.

"Well done, you two! I knew you could do it,"
said Murkbag, relieved at finding familiar
ground. He tossed the inkpot playfully from one
hand to the other, and the goblins could see he
hadn't noticed it was different from the one he'd
given them earlier.

Murkbag continued twirling the inkpot

around as he spoke, a little absentmindedly, thought Pungent.

"I don't know what took you so long, out there," Murkbag was saying, "but the result is the important thing, and, well, here we are – all bottled and safe!"

He tossed the inkpot even higher in the air, just as he snagged his trailing robe on a thorn bush. With a yelp he was pulled off balance.

Stinglip opened his mouth in surprise, wondering why

Murkbag was suddenly dancing! He didn't see the flying inkpot until it was too late ... and it plugged him! He staggered backwards, slipped and fell, landing awkwardly.

Pungent was equally surprised, his ridiculous rabbit ears flopping about with every turn of the head. By the time he had wrestled one ear into each hand, both Murkbag and Stinglip were lying on the ground.

Murkbag sprang to his feet. He tried to laugh it off but found it difficult to hide his embarrassment as the contents of his robe spilled out, bouncing and leaking their way into the night.

Pungent turned to Stinglip, who hadn't got up yet. In fact, he was lying quite still.

"You all right, Stinglip?" Pungent asked. No response.

Pungent held out a gloved hand. "Come on, don't muck about."

Stinglip was still lying on his back – with, Pungent noticed, something in his mouth. He bent down and realised that it was the inkpot. He pulled it out, but the cork was missing! A single dark line of gloop was running down the side of Stinglip's cheek.

Pungent gasped.

Stinglip had *swallowed* the sheep's shadow!

Feeling Sheepish

Stinglip started to moan, slowly rolling his head back and forth. Pungent could hear Murkbag still rooting around in the darkness, mumbling something about pocket zips. He was about to call him over when Stinglip's eyelids flickered. He sat up so suddenly it made Pungent jump.

"Pungent, are you OK?" said Stinglip. "Why are you looking at me like that?"

"Am *I* OK?" said Pungent. "What about *you*?"

Stinglip frowned. "I'm fine – why?"

"Stinglip – you've just swallowed *this*." Pungent held up the empty inkpot.

"Do what?"

"You've just swallowed the sheep shadow from this pot! Don't you remember? Murkbag dropped the inkpot, er …" – he finished the explanation with a curve of his hand in the air – "and, er … into your mouth!"

Stinglip looked baffled. Pungent tried again.

"How do you feel?"

Stinglip frowned again and thought carefully. He scratched himself in a way Pungent had never seen a goblin scratch himself before, and said, "I … feel … *grr-reat*!"

Pungent gave him a strange look. He helped him to his feet and together they headed over to Murkbag.

"Aha! There you are," said Murkbag, still adjusting his pockets. "I think I've got everything,

most embarrassing, dropping everything like that.
Still, no harm done, eh?"

He flashed them a weak smile and raised a
foot as if to start walking, but stopped, the foot
dangling in mid-step. Pungent could see
Murkbag staring at Stinglip. He joined in, and
his jaw dropped a notch.

Stinglip was down on
all fours and appeared
to be chewing
the grass!

"He, um … does that often, does he?" said Murkbag, his foot deciding to finish off what it had started.

But Pungent found it difficult to answer. Fingering the inkpot in his hand he managed a shrug. He had a really bad feeling about this.

Stinglip, sensing a change in mood from the others, stopped chewing and got to his feet. "Right then," he grinned. "Which way are we going?"

Pungent winced. Maybe he should tell Murkbag what had happened in the field. If he admitted they had failed to steal a shadow properly, Murkbag was bound to be angry. On the other hand, they had *stolen* the inkpot – that had to count for something, right? But what would Murkbag say if he knew they had *lied* about it? Pungent swallowed hard and decided, for now, not to say anything.

That was the second mistake he made that night, and it wouldn't be the last.

Chapter Nine

Chasing Shadows

The three Shadow Goblins walked along briskly. Murkbag was keen to be back at Goat's Log. But Stinglip couldn't see what was the hurry. Everything smelt so *good*. The grass had seen better times, true – but the thistles and thickets and brambles that lined the path on both sides were in need of far more attention than Murkbag and Pungent were, apparently, prepared to give.

"Will you come *on*, back there!" said Murkbag with growing alarm at Stinglip's behaviour. "There's still a lot to do tonight, and we've lost so much time."

Pungent's knees felt weaker with every step he took. Stinglip's condition seemed to be getting worse. Perhaps he should own up now – the longer he waited before he told Murkbag, the worse it would be.

They could be expelled! Never get to be real Shadow Goblins! It didn't bear thinking about.

"Er, sir, can I say something?" Pungent started.

But Murkbag had stopped and was holding up a hand.

Puzzled, Pungent stopped.

For a moment he thought Stinglip was doing something … sheepish.

But no. A shadow had appeared in front of them. It had no definite shape to it, and hung about in the air above their heads. It seemed to be *watching* them … *listening*!

He felt a tug behind him. A sudden tearing noise made him wheel around. Stinglip was on all fours again, munching on Pungent's rabbit-tail.

"What are you *doing*?" hissed Pungent. "Can't you see what's happening?"

He turned back around to see that the shadow had started to move towards them.

"*RUN!*" shouted Murkbag. He grabbed Pungent by the ears and Stinglip by a *tail* and, despite the panic, he found time to wonder, *funny, haven't noticed that before!*

And then they were running, back down the path the way they had come, and back into the heart of Black Wood, the last place they wanted to go!

Pungent couldn't look behind him in his rabbit costume, so he took Murkbag's word for it when he gasped, "It's getting closer – we'll have to s-split up!"

Murkbag was having a bad night! He'd had a bad feeling when the class began, and he was definitely having a bad feeling about the shapeless shadow chasing them now.

But he was supposed to be the one in charge, so he had to try to keep a clear head. And, most of all, not to p-p-panic!

"Get back to Goat's Log," he panted. "It's hollowed out one end – inside you'll find a map to a place called The Tree of Shadows – you'll be safe there!"

Pungent
tried to say
something, but
Murkbag was
shouting now. "I'll
**try and hold it off –
now GO!"**

Pungent and Stinglip
were flung off the path
and rolled into a tangled
heap in the darkness.
They helped each other
up and ran away from
the path, crashing through

the undergrowth, hoping to find some way to double back on themselves and to the safety of Goat's Log.

They saw and heard nothing more and after a while they slowed to a trot and then a walk, convinced, at last, that the immediate danger had passed.

"What *was* that thing?" gasped Stinglip.

"I've no idea," said Pungent. They finally stopped and sank to their knees, gulping in air.

"D'you think it was the same thing that was in the field?"

"Could be – only we didn't see it, did we. But, yeah, it *felt* the same … y'know?"

Stinglip nodded.

Slowly, they regained their breath and then a thought occurred to both of them at the same time. They looked at each other and said …

"Murkbag!"

A Rattle of Bones!

T here was no doubt Murkbag had saved
them from the shadow.

"We have to find him," said Pungent.

"He may have got to Goat's Log anyway. It
makes sense to start there, right?" suggested
Stinglip. They got to their feet and tried to work
out where they might be.

They soon realised they were lost.

"All we can do is start walking in a straight
line and hope we find the path – what d'you
reckon, Stinglip? *Stinglip?*"

There was a rustling sound from behind a
nearby tree.

"Are you eating leaves again?"

Pungent walked round the tree and let out a yelp. A sheep gazed up at him. Stinglip's robe hung around it in tatters. Shreds of material, trousers and shoes scattered the floor.

"Baa!" said the sheep.

"S-s-stinglip?"

Of course, Pungent knew that Stinglip was behaving the way he was as a result of swallowing the gloop from the inkpot. But somehow he had persuaded himself that his friend's behaviour was

temporary, that it would wear off after a couple of hours, and he would be back to his old ways.

But as Pungent looked down at him now, he knew that Stinglip would *not* be going back to his own ways. Not for some time!

And then, if things weren't bad enough, Pungent could hear another noise, zigzagging its way towards them.

He had no idea which direction it was coming from, and felt that any of the surrounding trees could be hiding some terrible creature, just waiting to pounce. So he squatted down next to Stinglip, keeping very still and very, very quiet. He hoped Stinglip would do the same.

As the buzzing noise closed in around them, Pungent thought he could make out a definite shape this time. He was expecting to see the shapeless shadow, but instead a thin, white figure was picking its way through the brambles. He gulped. What he saw was very thin, and very white. To his horror he realised it was a *skeleton*!

Pungent turned to Stinglip and brought a trembling finger to his lips.

"Baa!" said Stinglip.

Pungent could have cried. The skeleton stopped and stared in their direction.

Pungent held his breath … Stinglip didn't.

"Baa!" he said again, and trotted out into the open.

The figure made a funny noise when it saw Stinglip, possibly a laugh, then made its way directly towards them.

Pungent's mind was racing. If only he wasn't wearing this ridiculous costume then he could …

The rabbit costume – of *course*! He could hypnotise the skeleton! He closed his eyes and counted to three …

With a squeal, Pungent pounced. Eyes still tightly shut he jiggled a jig, hopped and bopped and sang the Ibble Obble song.

Murkbag would have been proud of him. He was a crazy bouncing rabbit and he didn't care who knew it!

The skeleton was clearly caught off guard and staggered backwards, making a noise like a bee with hiccups. He fell over and carried on paddling backwards – all bones and rattle!

Pungent was so surprised at the effect his dancing was having that he stopped. The skeleton, for his part, kept on going until he was a good distance away.

The skeleton still didn't try and stand up. It just sat there … buzzing.

The skeleton's skull turned slowly away from Pungent and he realised it was watching Stinglip, who was apparently bored of watching skeletons clattering about the place, and had turned his attention back to food.

Pungent was feeling hot and prickly inside his hot and prickly rabbit costume, and he wasn't quite sure what to do next.

The skeleton stood up, brushed himself down and walked boldly towards Pungent. He held out a hand and grinned a skeleton grin.

"Hi there, my name's Bone-zzz!"

Chapter Eleven

Bone-zzz

Pungent was so shocked by the skeleton's unexpected friendliness that he smiled stiffly and shook the bony hand. The skeleton's bones jangled so much, Pungent feared he was about to collapse and said, "Oh, sorry, um …" Bone-zzz grinned again and Pungent managed to mumble his name by way of reply.

"Must say," said Bone-zzz, "you gave me quite a scare – sent the shivers right through me!" He giggled and tapped his ribs encouragingly, waiting for Pungent to join in with the joke.

Pungent was still struggling to find the right words. The skeleton seemed to notice.

"Aw, don't mind me, I'm a joke a minute. Well, you have to be, looking the way I do!" This time he tapped his skull with his knuckles, making a sound like a hollow coconut.

"Sorry," said Pungent. "It's just I was, um … expecting to shout a lot and run away!"

Bone-zzz roared. "Nice one! … hehe … like it, *run away*, yeah … hehe!" He stopped laughing suddenly and sighed. "Actually, wouldn't blame you there." He looked over both shoulders as if checking they were alone. "There's all sorts going on in here. Some of it good, some of it bad!"

"P-p-pungent," came a small voice, "c-c-can we go now?" Stinglip was standing in the middle of a bush, picking bits of leaf out of his mouth and looking very uncomfortable. He had managed to find most of his clothes, though he

68

seemed a little confused about the bite marks.

"Stinglip, you're back!" said Pungent
with relief. He turned to Bone-zzz
and was about to try and
explain the sudden change
in his friend, but Bone-zzz
beat him to it.

"A shape-shifting
sheep, I see. You're
not the first, won't be
the last!"

"You *know* about
him?" asked Pungent in
surprise.

"Well, it doesn't take
much to figure it out,
now does it?"

Pungent somehow knew he could trust
Bone-zzz. They went a short distance to a shelter
made of sticks and bones, found a comfortable
spot, and Pungent told Bone-zzz everything.

Bone-zzz listened to every word. He
looked excited when
Pungent mentioned the
mysterious shadow, but
waited patiently until he
had finished.

"That shadow you been
running away from – that'll
be mine!" said Bone-zzz
quietly.

"What, the great b-big
b-black thing that chases
everyone?" asked Stinglip.

"It doesn't mean to – it's only scared."

"*S-scared?*" said Stinglip.

Pungent looked at Bone-zzz.

The skeleton was fingering a small inkpot
that was attached to one of his ribs by a piece of

string. He looked sad and lost in his thoughts. "What happened, Bone-zzz? How come you're out here all on your own?"

The Story of Bone-zzz

Bone-zzz sighed. He leaned back and ran his fingers up and down his ribs like a xylophone. Immediately a fly buzzed to life and circled the inside of his rib cage.

"Well, first off, I'm a Shadow Goblin like you!" He smiled at their faces. "Thought that would surprise you! See my little friend here?" he said, pointing to the fly.

"Well, it all started with her, a while ago now. Don't ask when, because in here you soon forget about time!

"Much like you two I was having my first few lessons, you know, learning about the usual stuff.

All was going well, hand shadows fine, shadow-stealing fine, and I was ready to do my first shape-shift. For practice you have to gargle with ink and sing the Ibble Obble song at the same time – don't ask me why!

"Anyway, I'm gargling away when this fly comes buzzing out of nowhere and into my mouth! Well, next thing I knows, I'm coughing and choking and all sorts – and then, yeah, you guessed it – I swallow the ink, fly an' all!

"As your friend here knows," said Bone-zzz, nodding at Stinglip, "strange things can happen to a goblin if you swallow ink before you're good and ready!

"Well, my throat starts burning, like I'm on fire, and the teacher's flapping around and trying to get a bucket of water down me when, all of a sudden, BOOM!

"Yeah, that's it – I *explode*!

"Well, you can imagine – pandemonium. Only, when I stand up, they're all running away from me! Turns out, not only my shadow's gone … but all my bits!" Bone-zzz looked down at himself and rattled his bones.

"And you know the funny thing? I'm left with little missy here buzzin' around my insides – won't leave me for nothing! And, to be honest, I'm kinda glad. Keeps me company, see.

"Well, everyone pretends they don't mind – once they get over the look of me, like.

Only, I've got no shadow. Imagine that – a Shadow Goblin with no shadow! I mean, the *shame*!

"So after a while I decide I've got to try and find my shadow, but I don't know where to look. And then all this chasing stuff starts happening. I know it's *my* shadow, but I keep missing him!"

Pungent and Stinglip sat there, speechless.

"My shadow's out there somewhere! And I know it's looking for me, like I'm looking for it. Trouble is, if I don't find it soon and put it safely back in my inkpot, it's going to fade away." He held up the inkpot and smiled weakly.

They were all silent for a moment, and then Bone-zzz sighed heavily again and spoke so quietly the other goblins only just heard him. "It doesn't mean any harm, it's just scared that's all!"

Pungent patted a bony shoulder, carefully.

"But why does it chase after everyone?"

"Like I say, it's panicking. It knows it has to find me soon, so it's running around jumping on anyone it can find – just hoping."

"Then, why is it stealing shadows as well?" asked Stinglip.

Bone-zzz frowned, the way only a skeleton can. "What do you mean?"

Pungent explained about the inkpot they'd found.

Bone-zzz shrugged. "I just reckon it's so confused it doesn't know what it's doing." He scratched himself, bone on bone, and sighed.

"My only hope now is to try and find a place called The Tree of Shadows. That's where lost and found inkpots are kept. Maybe it's there, somewhere. Trouble is," he sniffed, "I've no idea where to find it."

But Pungent was already jumping to his feet. "The Tree of Shadows? Murkbag told us to meet him there. He said we'd be safe, do you remember, Stinglip? He said there's a hidden map inside Goat's Log, a map that'll take us to The Tree of Shadows."

And so the three friends – one in a rabbit costume, one a shape-shifting sheep and one a walking-talking skeleton – set off to find Goat's Log and the map that would help them find safety and a lost shadow.

The Map

Bone-zzz may not have known the whereabouts of The Tree of Shadows, but he knew exactly where to find Goat's Log.

Once there, they soon found a small round hole in the log, exactly as Murkbag had described. Bone-zzz snapped his left arm off and threaded it into the hole, poking it around like a stick!

"Don't worry," he said cheerfully. "It doesn't hurt, and I can fix myself back in a jiffy – done it loads of times!"

A bit more poking and then, "Aha! Got it!"

79

Pungent opened out the map and spread it out on the floor, trying not to listen to Bone-zzz clicking himself back together.

"Not much to it!" frowned Pungent. "There's Goat's Log here … and a bunch of trees," he turned around, "which must be those three over there!"

"Well," said Bone-zzz, "we're looking for The Tree of Shadows. The clue's going to be in the name … so it's gotta be one of them!"

Pungent was not impressed. For a start there was no obvious sign of Murkbag. Pungent was

hoping to see him holding up his gloved hands and smiling that silly grin of his. He looked at the trees and sighed.

One was far too thin, more stick than tree. The second was tiny. And the third, thought Pungent, was the worst of the lot. It was very, very old and had clearly seen better days. At some point in its eventful life, a fork of lightning must have given it a right going over! It stood there now, sad, silent … and hollow!

It only had three branches left and a trunk riddled with holes. In a better light, thought Pungent, you'd be able to see right through it. Pathetic!

Bone-zzz, however, was ready to believe anything and was busily examining each tree. His fly, sensing a change of mood, buzzed happily.

Together the goblins walked around the third tree, prodding as they did so.

Suddenly, a whiff of smoke trailed out of the top like a chimney. Another thread of smoke appeared out of one of the many holes around its middle. Then another, and another. Soon, the whole tree was smoking, as if it was on fire!

"This *can't* be it," said Pungent quietly, but somehow he knew it was. He had expected a giant tree. A tree of intimidation. A tree that said, "*Look at me and weep*" not "*Gosh it's smoky in here, can somebody open a window?*"

The Tree of Shadows

"So what *is* The Tree of Shadows?" asked Pungent, waving a hand in front of his face.

"It's the place where shadows are kept – stored, if you like – a kind of library that we can come to and borrow from. But we're only told where it is when we're fully trained Shadow Goblins. And it's also a place where Lost Shadows come," said Bone-zzz. "They are all stored here and wait to be reclaimed."

"But why doesn't your shadow come here and wait for you?"

Bone-zzz shrugged. "I'm hoping it is! If it knows how to get here, if it *wants* to be here –

who knows what a shadow is thinking!"

The Tree of Shadows was really smoking by now and both Pungent and Bone-zzz were wondering if they should do something.

"Where's Stinglip?" asked Pungent. He realised he hadn't seen him for a while … since he had started to come over all sheepish again.

"I thought I saw him over there," said Bone-zzz, pointing to a tree stump. On it was a pile of familiar clothes. A row of bite-sized holes ran neatly down both trouser legs. Stinglip, however, was nowhere to be seen.

Suddenly a muffled voice could be heard coming from the burning tree. It didn't sound worried at all. In fact, it sounded quite cross.

"Typical, absolutely *typical*," it was saying. "There's nothing else for it. I'll have to take the whole lot out and start again!"

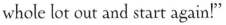

There followed the clinking
of inkpots. Then out of the
black fog appeared a little
Monkey Goblin, weighed
down by a tower of inkpots
which looked as though they
would fall at any moment.
She was unaware of her
audience and began setting
down the inkpots in neat
little rows, counting
quietly to herself.

Pungent and
Bone-zzz
were still
trying to

decide whether

or not to

interrupt her concentration,

when she looked up.

"Ah, *there* you are!" said the

Monkey Goblin, and then

frowned. "I say, where are your

buckets? You'll need buckets for the water,

and you'll need water for the fire. Because that fire

in there is going to keep on licking – and mark my

words you don't want no licking fire, oh no!"

With that, she turned and disappeared into the

swirls of smoke. When she came out again, a few

minutes later, she was coughing and her face was

blackened by the soot, but she still seemed

untroubled. If anything, she was balancing more

inkpots than before.

She addressed them without looking up.

"You two still here? I'd get a move on if I were you, or we'll have the whole lot down on us and then where will we be?" She lined up the inkpots and stood, hands on hips. "One more trip should do."

Just then Stinglip came crashing out of the trees. He was followed quickly by Murkbag, and then the black shadow! There was plenty of screaming all round, as you would expect.

As Stinglip ran past Pungent and Bone-zzz, he changed from Stinglip the Shadow Goblin ... to a sheep!

His eyes were wild and his shouts turned to bleats of alarm. So intent was he in trying to escape the shadow, he didn't see the rows and rows of inkpots, and blundered through them, smashing and spilling them in all directions!

Dancing Shadows

It would be fair to say that the Monkey
Goblin was not happy. She didn't say it, in so
many words, but the screaming was
a clue. Then there was the
hair pulling (her
own), and the dribbling.
Oh yes, dribbling is a *sure*
sign of an unhappy Monkey
Goblin.

"Me pots!" she wailed.
"Look at all me pots!" It was
all she could say, over
and over again.

Stinglip, unaware of the damage he had caused, had now reached the trees on the far side and disappeared from view.

The shadow stopped quite suddenly, quivering with effort. It was thinner now, and less black ... almost transparent.

Pungent was aware of a buzzing sound and saw Bone-zzz hopping up and down, pointing excitedly.

"Me, me, me," he chuckled. "That be me, me, me!"

Ignoring the scattered inkpots, he ran to the shadow and ... held out his bony arms. They wrapped themselves around each other, a swirling embrace of smoke and bones! The only sound was the buzzing of the fly, as happy as a purring cat.

Meanwhile, the shadows were stirring!

The spilt and broken inkpot shadows were running together, dancing, twisting and curling. The poor Monkey Goblin was desperately running around trying to put them back in their pots, but it was no use.

Eventually, aware of their freedom, the shadows melted away into the trees.

"This is bad," groaned the Monkey Goblin, "this is very, very bad!" At last, with a fistful of empty inkpots still in each hand, she slumped to the floor, exhausted.

Murkbag, meanwhile, had put out the fire. Now he was trying his best to catch the few remaining shadow-stragglers.

Throughout all of this Pungent had been so shocked by what he witnessed that he had done more or less nothing. He shook his head in shame. Stinglip was nowhere to be seen, so he went over to comfort the Monkey Goblin.

She was muttering darkly to herself and appeared to be packing a selection of burned and charred bottles of ointments, dishes, and test-tubes of various lengths, wrapping them all up in a small spotted cloth.

"I'm off, me! I told them! No more hot smoky shadows – they *always* catch fire in the end! I told them all, NO … MORE! It'll take *years* to get them lot back – if they last that long, which I doubt! Most will probably go up in a poof of smoke anyway."

When she had tied her bundle to a stick, she swung it over a shoulder and padded off into the woods, muttering to herself. "Shadow Goblins, *paf!*

Plonkers, the lot of
them. I should
have gone to
work with
those nice-looking
dwarves in
the next
valley …"
Pungent

shrugged and went back to The Tree of Shadows.
It was still smoking, but with a hiss of dampness
about it. Murkbag emerged, grinning broadly,
with a dripping bucket and waving an inkpot.

"That should do it!" Wiping his brow, he
looked at Pungent. "You found this place all
right, I see?" His face was black with soot and
thin wisps of smoke trailed off him.

"Sir," said Pungent, "I'm really sorry but—"

"If you're going to tell me about Stinglip drinking the gloop, then don't worry, I already know!"

"But how did you …?"

"I figured it out – wasn't too difficult. Stinglip with a sheep's tail was one clue, chewing the grass another." Murkbag looked serious for a minute.

"But, yes, you should have told me."

"What will happen to him? I mean, er … will he be OK?"

"Probably, eventually, but these things take time. You'll have to watch him. Well, we'll both watch him."

Pungent nodded.

"But, you know the first thing we gotta do?" He turned and waved a hand at the inky mess that lay sprawled out around them. "We got to clean up this mess and we got to get into those woods and catch as many of those shadows as we can."

"But the Monkey Goblin said it would take years."

"*Nah!* Three days at the most! Shadows soon realise they need their inkpots!"

Pungent nodded.

"What I want to know," said Murkbag, "is how that black shadow managed to put another shadow into an inkpot? Beats me."

Just then Stinglip-the-sheep appeared. He was only mildly curious about the mess that lay sprawled out before him. He caught the scent of some blueberry-thorn leaves – and trotted off to find them.

Bone-zzz joined them, clutching his inkpot in both hands. "Great day! Great, great day!" he was saying. His tummy-fly buzzed a happy buzz.

The Adventure Begins!

"**R**eady, everyone?" asked Murkbag.

The others nodded.

So Murkbag and his swishy *Robe of Darkness*,
Pungent and his rabbit costume, Stinglip, half
Shadow Goblin, half sheep, and Bone-zzz, the
walking-talking buzzy skeleton, all headed off
into the shadows of Black Wood.

Armed with a sack of empty inkpots and a
bunch of shadow nets, they spent two weeks
catching every last one of the missing shadows.

The adventures, the drama and the scares that
followed them during that time in Black Wood
are not for this book. They are so shocking in

their eye-watering terror that I'm not sure you would believe them. It is enough to know that the missing shadows are safely back in their inkpots and stacked in neat little piles in The Tree of Shadows.

Murkbag is back teaching the cunning and fascinating ways of the Shadow Goblins. Pungent is *still* wearing the rabbit costume (he quite likes it now – just as well, because he's still rubbish at hand shadows). Stinglip is now more Shadow Goblin than sheep, but there is a chance he will never be the same again. And Bone-zzz, reunited with his shadow, was as buzzy as ever.

And the Monkey Goblin? Well, she did saunter over into the next valley. But dwarves are no substitute for goblins – ask the bears, they'll tell you – and she returned to The Tree of Shadows within the week.

As for The Tree of Shadows, you would never have known about the fire to look at it. Except perhaps for the hissing black smoke that for some reason won't go away.

But the Monkey Goblin likes that. She thinks it gives the place a bit of atmosphere. The hissing, broody Tree of Shadows looks out at you from Black Wood. A crack of a smile on its rough old bark, and a gaze that says, *"Hey – Look at me and weep!"*

Afterword

As far as I know, there have been no known cases of Shadow Goblins shape-shifting into children. However, just because I have not heard of such a thing, that's no guarantee it doesn't happen.

My advice? Keep away from unusual creatures singing silly songs and prancing around in rabbit costumes.

And I just hope you never see a friend or family member slowly changing shape, into some kind of, well you know ... *goblin*.

The Beginner's Guide to Hand Shadows

Can you guess what they are? Answers at the bottom of the page.

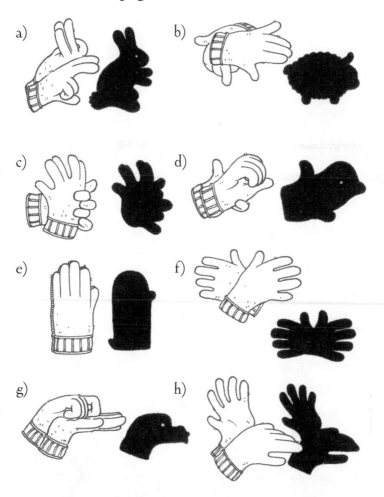

a)
b)
c)
d)
e)
f)
g)
h)

ENJOYED THIS BOOK?

Find out about the other books in the

GOBLINS

series from the website

www.hiddengoblins.co.uk

You can learn about the different characters,
download and print off fun activities
and games, and discover more about
the author, David Melling.

See you there!

stone GOBLINS

tree GOBLINS

puddle GOBLINS

shadow GOBLINS

Can you think of any other kinds of goblin?

David Melling would love to know about your ideas.

Send us a drawing or painting of your goblin, and tell us his or her name.

As well as seeing your picture up on the goblins website, you could win a fantastic goblin goody bag.

We will choose two winners per month.

Send your drawing to:
Goblins Drawing Competition

UK Readers:
Hodder Children's Books
338 Euston Road
London NW1 3BH

Australian Readers:
Hachette Children's Books
Level 17/207 Kent Street
Sydney NSW 2000

New Zealand Readers:
Hachette Livre NZ Ltd
PO Box 100 749
North Shore City 0745

a goblin appetizer

Look out for those
**puddle
GOBLINS**